SKUNK
FOR
A DAY

Roger <u>C</u>aras
pictures by
Diane Paterson

Windmill Books, Inc.
and E. P. Dutton & Co., Inc.
New York

For J. P., R. vG., E. E., L. H., W. W. and S. L.

Text copyright © 1976 by Roger Caras
Illustrations copyright © 1976 by Diane Paterson
All rights reserved
Published by Windmill Books & E. P. Dutton & Co.
201 Park Avenue South, New York, New York 10003

Library of Congress Cataloging in Publication Data
Caras, Roger A Skunk for a day.

SUMMARY: *Follows the activities of a young skunk*
from nightfall till dawn as he forages for food.

1. Skunks—Juvenile literature. [1. Skunks—Habits and behavior] I. Paterson, Diane
II. Title.

QL737.C25C37   1976   599'.74447   75-25827
ISBN 0-525-61537-7

Published simultaneously in Canada by Clarke, Irwin & Company, Limited,
Toronto and Vancouver
Designed by The Etheredges
Printed in the U.S.A.   First Edition
10 9 8 7 6 5 4 3 2 1

Today you are a skunk. Not a little spotted skunk—not a big hooded skunk with an all-white back—and not a heavy hog-nosed skunk with (naturally) a pig-like nose. You are a small, neat, shiny black-and-white striped skunk with a white streak down your nose and a white patch on the top of your head. That patch divides over your shoulders and runs down your body in two stripes that end up as fringes on your feathery tail. All-in-all, you are a rather handsome little animal.

You have other names besides *striped skunk,* of course. Some people call you *polecat,* some people call you *wood pussy* and some people call you *phoby cat.* You are even called *civet,* although a civet is another kind of animal from the other side of the world. (People sometimes get confused when it comes to animal names.) Scientists call you *Mephitis* and that is a Latin word that means *a terrible smell that rises up from the ground.* You do, in fact, smell pretty bad to the rest of the world. That doesn't bother you, though. In the world where you live almost everything is busy trying to eat everything else much of the time. You smell so bad, almost no other animal will even come close, much less try to turn you into his supper. And besides, other skunks seem to enjoy your smell. That all adds up to a nice long life and a skunk mate when you are old enough to have one. Not a bad arrangement at all.

Your day began much the way all skunk days begin—just at night-fall—so we might say TONIGHT you are a skunk. You are what is known as a *nocturnal* animal which means you feel better about things when it is dark. All over the countryside, just as the sun begins to set, skunks shuffle out from hollow logs, out from under wind-toppled trees and old abandoned buildings. Some move up from underground burrows. They come out to begin the adventures of the skunk's world of night.

When you were born you and your six brothers and sisters all together didn't even weigh a half-pound. You had been growing inside your mother (she was just a year old herself then) for sixty-three days, but that is as big as you got before you were born. You weighed one ounce each. Your eyes were closed, and for seven weeks you lived on your mother's milk. Then she began to teach you and your litter-mates how to hunt. Each night you all set off after her in a pretty straight line. And as your new night begins, that is what is on your little skunk mind—all the good things you learned to eat as you trailed behind your mother.

On this particular night your wanderings take you close to a farm. You don't only eat animal food. You are quite pleased with an apple, a carrot, a melon or any other crop you can harvest. As you move across the still, dark farm your nose tells you corn is stored nearby, and you move in for a bit of that, as well. Just beyond the corncrib there is a henhouse and that comes next. You are doing what all skunks do when they are not sleeping—you are eating. Skunks look like stuffed toys because skunks are stuffed just about all of the time.

Now, henhouses are not good skunk ideas. (Skunks don't really have ideas, of course, but it is still "bad news" when a skunk gets near a farmer's hens.) As a skunk, you will eat the hens' eggs and then quite probably their chicks and possibly even part of a hen or two. That makes farmers feel insecure and unhappy, and farm dogs are trained to be very noisy when their sensitive noses tell them that a skunk has come too close.

From beside the farm house a terrible racket begins. A dog is chained to the porch railing, and he has sensed your presence. (That is one bad thing about smelling like a skunk—it is hard to pretend that you are not there!) The dog is barking and leaping about, and inside the house the lights come on. Pulling on his pants, the farmer rushes from his bedroom, grabbing his big double-barrelled shotgun. Just as he steps out the door, the old porch railing tears loose, and the farm dog is heading across the yard yapping and yowling and dragging a piece of the broken rail behind him. The farmer whistles and calls and then starts out after the dog, still hitching up his pants as he goes.

All of this doesn't really frighten you, and although you are seldom in a hurry to get any place you do shuffle off away from the noise. It displeases you, for as a nighttime animal you generally like things to be quiet and peaceful. There is nothing very peaceful about the fuss you have stirred up by snooping around the henhouse. Even the hens are carrying on by now, and a rooster who thinks it must be morning is sitting up on a fence making a fool of himself by calling to a sun that isn't up yet. You just keep shuffling off toward the woods. Unfortunately, because you are a skunk, you leave a distinct trail behind. It isn't very difficult for a dog to follow, even a dog dragging a hunk of farmhouse behind him.

All of this noise, and having your supper rudely disturbed, has not done very much for your disposition. There is a whole variety of sounds you can make, and you start down the list now. As you amble along you twitter. Still the dog keeps coming, the farmer keeps shouting and the cock keeps crowing. So you growl. Then you chhurrrrrrrrr a little bit, and then you chhhattter and scold. The noise doesn't stop and, in fact, the dog is getting closer and louder, so you try several different sounds all at once. You seem to enjoy mumbling to yourself, mumbling and grumbling.

As you move out of the farmer's yard, you pass between two trees that are only a foot or so apart. Naturally, the farm dog follows your trail and squeezes between the trees, too. That is when you hear him yelp! The piece of porch railing which was bouncing along the ground behind him has turned sideways and won't pass through the opening. He is stuck and very angry. You can hear that he has stopped coming, and you wait a moment and listen. All of this has made you hungry again, so you start turning over rocks to see what you can find. But that is not where your farmyard adventure is going to end. The farmer has come panting up behind the dog and stops to free the piece of porch rail from the trees. He wants to lead his dog home before it gets into trouble, but the dog bursts away and is on your trail again. Now you *are* angry!

Because you are a skunk you would rather move away than fight, but you can only be pushed so far, and that is about as far as you have already been pushed. As the dog comes around a large tree to where you are busy minding your own beetle grubs, you go into battle posture. First you stamp your feet. If the dog were smart, he would take the hint and move away—quietly.

Your foot-stamping didn't do it, so you flip your tail up high over your back and hold it there like a widespread fan. Its white fringes shine in the moonlight that is coming down through the trees. The foolish dog is now snarling and starting to come closer.

You have no choice at this point, so you arch your back and flip up into a dainty, graceful handstand. You aren't doing it to be graceful, though, for now your very life is being threatened. You move about on your front paws, your hind feet tucked in and your tail still arched forward. You wait. The dog is foolish enough to keep coming, low to the ground and snarling. That is it! All of your skunk patience has been used up. When the dog is a little over twelve feet away, you give him two short blasts with the twin nozzles under your tail. The battle is over. You hit the dog with a very fine spray of a yellowish, oily material, nothing much more than a fine mist, but his nose and eyes felt instantly on fire.

The farmer is still huffing-and-puffing along behind, and his nose plus the dog's shriek tell him what has happened. He says some very unpleasant things about skunks for now he will have to lock his dog in a shed for the night and then head down to the market in the morning. It is going to be expensive, because the only thing that will remove your mark from his dog is tomato juice! It will take cans and cans of tomato juice and bath after bath, and even after all of that is done the dog will still smell a little like you every time it rains. That can last for months. The farmer will also have to burn the clothes he is wearing when he washes his dog. It is little wonder that you are not considered the farmer's best friend.

Now it is quiet again. The farmer has headed back to his own yard, because he knows it is dangerous for him to go stumbling around in the dark. Once a skunk is angry, he is likely to let go at anyone who approaches, and it is quite obvious to him you are angry. The farmer mutters to himself as he walks, and his dog slinks along behind, whining and looking ashamed of himself.

Of course, all this has made you hungry, so you start exploring around the roots of a tree that had been blown down in a storm. There are endless hiding places in a tangle like that, and in your own patient way you start going through them one after another. Beetles and grubs, a small garter snake and some tender plant bulbs reward your effort. You keep right on nibbling and munching along, when a very soft sound attracts your attention. It is so faint a human being probably wouldn't hear it at all, but your ears have been designed differently. The sound is coming from above, and you recognize it.

You move in among some tangled roots and are very still. The almost-impossibly soft sound you heard was the wind moving through the hushed wings of a great horned owl. All owls have very soft feathers on their wings to keep them silent as they hunt and glide at night. But you heard the almost-impossible, and that is why you froze. The great owl thrust its powerful feet out in front and grasped a branch jutting out from a tree not far away. It heard your scratching as you dug for the next course of your all-night dinner, and it moved in to see if you could be captured. Hunting by ear and by sight when it can detect movement, even on the darkest night, the great horned owl now must depend on you to move. As long as you are absolutely still, it can't see you and you will make no noise. So you remain in among the roots, and the owl tires of the waiting game and swishes away in search of less-wary prey. It is the night-game of the silent hunter and the silent prey. This time you won.

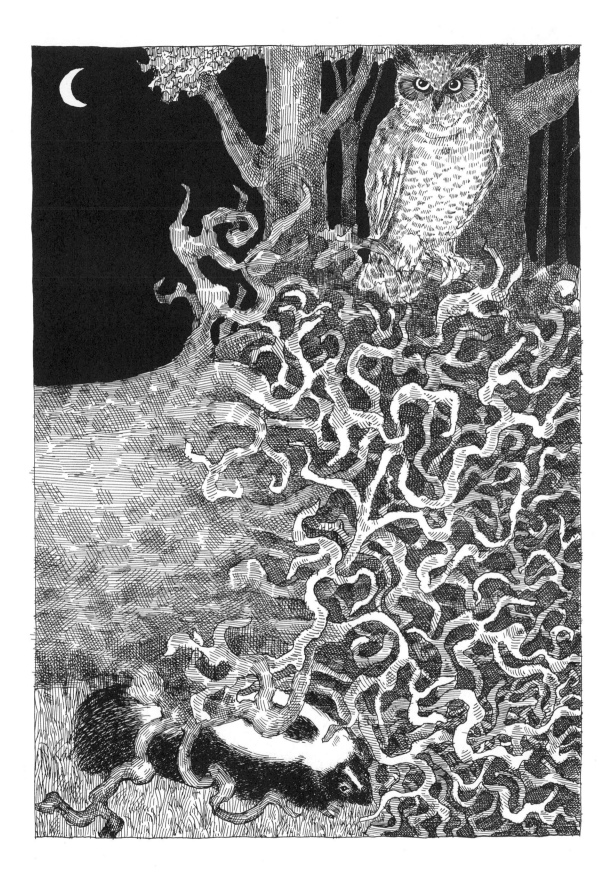

Except for the little extra excitement with the farm dog, this hasn't been an unusual night. Now that things have quieted down and both the dog and the owl are behind you, you settle down again to the very serious business of eating. You scratch away as you move along, cooing softly to yourself when you find something that tastes particularly good, which is just about everything. You use your front paws like little human hands, touching, turning, picking things through. As you move away from the farm, you come to a pond. Although you can swim if you have to, it is not the sort of thing you do for pleasure. So you move around the pond and munch on a haunch of frog along the way. Several other green frogs hop away, and a very large bullfrog gurrrompppppps from too far out in the pond for you to go unless you swim after him.

After you check out the pond (it is a place you come to every few nights or so because you do have regular trails you follow), you come to an open field. The great horned owl is probably still around, so you stick close to some bushes that are growing along the fence that closes the pasture in on all four sides. Out in the open you could always do your handstand and drive off just about any other animal in the world, but that old owl could still swoop down on you and you could become a meal.

As a skunk you learn some things from experience. First there were the early expeditions with your mother, with all of the little skunks in a row, and then there were the things you learned when you moved off on your own. One of those lessons was that some animals are careless on the highway. Whenever you hear the sounds of cars and trucks roaring by and see their great yellow lights poking holes in the dark, you move toward them. Before long, experience has taught you, you will come upon the remains of a careless rabbit or opossum, and even that pleases you as the next course in your long meal.

The fact that your weapon—your spray—is so very powerful protects you from nearly all enemies. Aside from foolish dogs and silent-winged great horned owls, almost no living creature will go near you —except another skunk who will coo and whistle and eventually, perhaps, be your mate. But your special power also works against you at times. You find it very difficult to understand that anything will seriously challenge your right-of-way. You can learn from the things you have seen that other animals can die on the road, but not that you can be one of them. That is something skunks are unable to figure out until it is too late.

You move along the soft, bushy shoulder of the road looking for treasures to cap your supper. Behind you the sky begins to lighten, and little pink and orange fingers creep up and out from under some soft, low-lying clouds. It will soon be morning again. Ahead you smell something and begin to move toward the scene of a tragic encounter between a large bus and a careless rabbit. As you shuffle and roll up onto the tar of the road surface, a truck rapidly rounds a curve. Like a huge ball of thunder, it swoops toward you. The noise is so startling and the headlights so sudden and blinding that you hardly have time to react.

Not all skunks will be as fortunate as you are this night. The truck misses you by inches. In your excitement you hit it twice with jets of scent. The rushing wind of the passing truck actually blows you off the road. You spin around and roll over twice before coming up against the root-tangle of a bush. The truck is gone into the night along with all the other threats and adventures. The dawn is moving rapidly up across the sky, and you have eaten enough for one night. Moving off into the bushes, you come at last to a hollow log, where you can feel safe and secure until a darkening sky and faint signals from your greedy stomach will tell you it is again time to begin the skunk's night of feeding. It is day now, a quiet time for skunks all across the land.